little Archie's
LUCKY DAY

ART BALTAZAR & FRANCO

Publisher / Co-CEO: Jon Goldwater
Co-President / Editor-In-Chief: Victor Gorelick
Co-President: Mike Pellerito
Co-President: Alex Segura
Chief Creative Officer: Roberto Aguirre-Sacasa
Chief Operating Officer: William Mooar
Chief Financial Officer: Robert Wintle
Director of Book Sales & Operations: Jonathan Betancourt
Production Manager: Stephen Oswald
Art Director / Production: Vincent Lovallo
Editor / Production: Jamie Lee Rotante
Co-CEO: Nancy Silberkleit

Little Archie
sleeps in his room
by the big oak
tree.

"ZZZ..." says
Little Archie.

"ZZZ..." purrs
the little red cat in
the big oak tree.

The little red cat awakes to greet his new friend.

A noise comes from outside!
Startled, the little red cat finds a place to hide!

Little Archie's mom doesn't notice the furry red rascal in the laundry basket.

"It's time to get ready for school! Don't forget your art project like you did last week!" says Little Archie's mom.

"Who are you?" asks Little Archie.

"Hey! I've been looking for this! You've found my favorite shirt!" Little Archie exclaims.

"You must be my good luck charm! I'm going to call you 'Red'!" cheers Little Archie.

Little Archie leaves to start his day... but it looks like he's forgetting something!

Little Archie goes to Riverdale Elementary School.

"What lessons will I learn today?!" he wonders.

Little Archie's classmates, Little Betty,
Little Veronica and Little Reggie hand in their
drawings to their teacher, Ms. Grundy.

"Oh no! I left my
drawing at home!"
Little Archie explains.

"Sorry, Little Archie. You'll have
to go sit in time out... again."
Ms. Grundy instructs.

Little Archie is **not** having a good day.

Little Betty and Little Veronica visit
their friend in time out.

Just as Little Archie begins to feel lonely, the little red cat appears!

With his new friend by his side, Little Archie notices that his time out is over!

"Wow, Red! You really must be my lucky charm! You made the time go by so quickly!" he exclaims.

WALK

WALK

Little Archie leaves time out and sees his good pal Little Jughead.

"Do you want to go play?" asks Little Jughead.

"No thanks, Little Jughead. I've got to see what else my cat Red can do!" responds Little Archie.

Red leads Little Archie outside.

Little Archie plays with Red, missing out on a
fun and tasty treat with Little Jughead.

Little Archie goes home to show his mom his new feline friend and good luck charm.

"You're home early! You usually play with Little Jughead at this time," says Little Archie's mom.

"Not today! It's been crazy! First I found my favorite shirt and then I forgot my art project and went to time out but it was fine because of my new best friend! We've been having so much fun!" exclaims Little Archie.

"That's nice, sweetie. But remember, you already have such good friends!"

"...You've been playing all day, now go wash up!" Little Archie's mom replies.

As Little Archie
washes up, Red
appears at his side.

"You may be my good luck
charm, but I shouldn't forget
about the other great friends
I have," says Little Archie.

Red leaps back into
his hiding place.

"Silly cat! I think it's time
for you to go back home,
to your own friends."
laughs Little Archie.

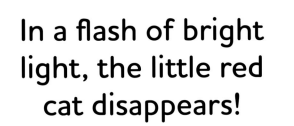

In a flash of bright light, the little red cat disappears!

"Goodbye, my lucky charm. Maybe I'll see you again someday!" Little Archie thinks to himself.

Later, Little Archie meets Little Jughead at the park.

"Hey, Little Jughead. I'm sorry I didn't play with you earlier," Little Archie apologies.

"That's okay, Little Archie! As long as we're friends, there's always time to play!" Little Jughead replies.

"Now, let's all get milkshakes with our pals!" suggests Little Jughead.

And that was when Little Archie realized that he was the lucky one, to have such **great** friends!